Return of the
Dragons

Return of the Dragons

Deborah Lee

Library of Congress Control Number: 2021920586
ISBN: Hardcover   978-1-6641-1035-9
                 Softcover   978-1-6641-1034-2
                 eBook   978-1-6641-1033-5

Print information available on the last page.

Rev. date: 10/05/2021

To order additional copies of this book, contact:
Xlibris
844-714-8691
www.Xlibris.com
Orders@Xlibris.com
833804

Chapter 1

Weapons in hand, Josh hiked up the hill through the long grass and headed toward his favorite spot. While he walked, he listened to the river as it gurgled and bubbled over rocks and stones while it flowed downstream. A strange uneasiness came over him that he had not felt since the Black Dragon had disappeared. Josh listened to the chatter of the squirrels, and birds call to one another.

As he crested the hill, Josh heard a splash and glanced at the river. Sure enough, his yellow retriever, Boomer, dove in after a duck. Josh laughed and walked toward the giant oak tree just as a flock of ducks flew overhead.

Josh sat at the base of the oak and leaned back, with his other dog, Warrior, lying beside him. He gazed at the river. It was peaceful here. He looked around at the gnarled tree trunks partially showing the new spring underbrush. A flood of memories returned when he looked at the scorched and burned grove of timber on the other side of the river. It had been five peaceful years since anyone had seen any dragons.

A shudder ran through his body. He tried to block out the devastating loss of life by covering his rugged face with his huge, calloused hands, hoping the images would go away. The Black Dragon with its enormous wingspan had destroyed so much. Tears welled up in his eyes. The town of three hundred had been reduced to rubble and 150 survivors. The Black Dragon carried off his parents and sister. The other dragons only took livestock, wild animals, but this one . . . the screams . . . it was years before the nightmares lessened. Tears were running freely now. Josh gripped his spear tightly, hoping this would keep the images away. It did not.

Josh leaned back, remembering that night. It had taken time, but he and the rest of the men from the village had set the trap here.

"We need to destroy that monster," Carl shouted as blood ran down his arm from the gaping wound. He watched as the Black Dragon disappeared with its latest victim gripped in its massive claws. His screams still rang in their ears.

"Troy has seen its tracks at the base of the mountain by the river," stated Josh. "Gather all the men after everyone is moved into the tunnels, including the animals. Meet in the tunnel by the river."

Troy gathered all the frightened women and children and guided them into the tunnels while the rest of the men rounded up the livestock and brought in food, water, blankets, and weapons.

When everyone was in, the men went to meet Josh.

"Everyone is in, and we have brought all the weapons left," said Troy.

Taking a stick, Josh squatted down and drew a map in the dirt. "Here's the river. The hill is on the left, the mountain and grove of trees on the right. Going to take our best archers with me. The rest will use axes and swords when we get close. Troy, take six men with you. You have one chance. Throw your axes so they hit the dragon directly on the base of the skull, then retreat. If you can do it, the monster should rear and give us the opportunity; we need to aim at his heart or do some major damage. Then it be will chaos, so be ready. Meet back here at sundown. Get some rest."

At sunset, the men left the tunnel. They split into their two groups. Troy took his men and crossed the river by the village while Josh and his group watched and waited for them to cross. An owl hooted, the prearranged signal. He replied.

The long grass covered any noise they made. Josh could only hope Troy was having the same luck.

The hill proved more difficult as they avoided fallen branches and twigs. He led his men up the hill into a clearing. With silence, they spread throughout the clearing, putting their weapons in order. One of the men gave the owl sound. No response.

A cold chill ran down Josh's spine. *What had gone wrong?* All night sounds had ceased. *Troy, where are you?* There was no sound.

All at once, a rush of wind whipped the trees and water. As Josh's eyes adjusted to the dim light, he looked at his men. One man pointed at the mountain.

The Black Dragon was there. *Had he seen them coming?*

An owl hooted. The signal. Josh responded. They were safe. The heavy black clouds moved and revealed the stars. The beast landed! Josh stared at the dragon's immense size. It dwarfed everything, including the mountains.

The monster's razor-sharp teeth barely showed as it edged its way to the riverbank. A guttural growl sounded from deep within its scale-covered chest. The dragon dipped its foot into the water and swirled it around. It was mesmerizing.

To see it kill from the air, so contradictory, and now to see it up close and peaceful.

Josh wanted to study the dragon when it was like this. It would seem everyone wanted to do the same the same thing because Troy did not throw his weapon.

The dragon's spiked tail swished and tossed all the branches and trees out of the way. The Black Dragon took a drink, then continued to talk to its own reflection. Suddenly, the dragon jerked upright and sniffed the air. Its nostrils flared! The slender spikes on his narrow head stood upright. Beady eyes scanned the area.

Josh exhaled as he watched the dragon go back to its fascination with its reflection. He could trust Troy to commence the battle.

A long roar of pain and a stream of fire rocketed skyward. An ax had found its mark. The night was filled with the swish of arrows in flight, hitting their target and a roaring dragon spewing fire. Men shouted, ran, and rolled to get out of the way as they fired their weapons. The men surrounded the Black Dragon. Josh's dog, Warrior, caused more havoc for the dragon with his barking and biting.

Damage to the left wing was extensive. Someone threw a sword, and the wing hung limp. The tail swung around, and a man screamed in pain. Flames flew toward the grove of trees and branches, and trees caught fire.

Josh looked at the last of his weapons—three spears. He picked up one and ran to the edge of the clearing and threw it. The damage was minor but enabled one of the men to get away from that wicked tail. Again. This time, the spear was close to the heart, but not deep. Josh dove out of the way as flames spewed in his direction. A distraction, this time from the water. Carl threw his ax and hit the dragon in the left leg.

The Black Dragon reared as Josh grabbed his last spear. He leaned back and threw with every ounce of strength he had left. The spear hit between the protective scales around the dragon's heart and went deep. Blood gushed forth, and the Black Dragon howled in pain. But still the defiant dragon did not fall. The men lay wounded and exhausted in the carnage. The dragon tried to give one more blast of fire, but only the scream of a mortally wounded animal came forth. Its body was covered with blood, from broken arrows and gaping sword and ax wounds.

The dying dragon fluttered and clawed its way up the mountain, using its limp tail for balance. The men watched in awe and deepening respect until it was out of sight.

Was that monster dead? If he had more weapons and better aim . . . ? How had Warrior known when and where to come? What was that barking?

Chapter 2

A dog nuzzled Josh's face and then licked him and brought him back to reality. "Warrior. Thank you, my friend. Hope I don't have any more mornings like this."

Normally, sitting under the branches of the large tree brought comfort, but not today. He had a nightmare last night. Not a good sign.

He looked at Warrior sitting beside him. The scarred mongrel stared at him with intelligent brown eyes. Josh laid his spear across his lap and petted the multicolored dog. "Never did figure out where you came from, but I'm sure glad you did."

Josh scanned the area. "Well, we have been able to use the wood they knocked down. Before that, the river was impossible to cross." Not because of the water but because he was sure the dragons lived in the mountains, and he did not want his children on the other side of the river. Large pine trees were knocked across the river by dragon's tails, and some of the trees were made into a sturdy bridge wide enough for a wagon a couple of years ago. He made some of it into buildings, fences, and firewood. "Soon I'll actually have to cut a tree." Josh sighed.

The sunrise crested the mountains shimmering on the river, and deer came out of a stand of trees across from him. "I could shoot one and take home some fresh venison for my family," he said as he stretched his lithe frame and watched the deer graze in the open meadow. "It's good to see the wild animals on the increase and hear so many birds again."

A dog barked. Josh watched as deer's flags went up, and they turned as one and leaped away. Boomer swam across the river and ran after the departing deer. "Come here, boy," yelled Josh. Boomer looked at the departing deer, then his master, and ran back across the bridge, up the hill, and shook his wet body. "Good boy. Down, Boomer." The yellow retriever lay panting at his feet.

Squirrels chattered, birds screeched, and smaller animals gave warning signals. Warrior came alert, bolted over Josh, and raced down the hill.

Josh scrambled to get up as he grabbed his weapons. He raced to the edge of the hill. The stillness was overwhelming. A growl beside him told him something was wrong. Josh looked for any sign of where Warrior had gone.

"There! The grass is moving. Warrior is headed to the village."

Boomer snarled. Josh looked at him with a hollow feeling in the pit of his stomach. He turned back and stared in horror as a red dragon's head showed above the trees. "Boomer, go!"

Josh started to run but stumbled and fell down the hill. *My family, did they make it into the tunnels? Did the men . . . Come on, Josh. Hurry. I need wings for feet, not stone. The village seemed so far away. I can hear the animals, but no people. They must be safe.*

Josh reached the village inn and stopped to catch his breath. It was like a graveyard. He could not hear the animals anymore. His family? His heart was pounding so loud he was sure the dragon could hear it. He slipped to the ground, unable to stand after running two miles. *Need a drink. Need to find everyone.*

Strong arms picked Josh up, and Carl gave him a drink. Then he was taken to the river. The trees had blocked his view of what was happening, and disbelief briefly took hold of him. All the villagers, including his family, were assembled by the river. The children were playing with a young, wounded dragon.

"Your daughter found the young dragon and tried to help it by fixing its wing. The mother came looking for it. She hasn't done anything to anyone yet, and we have fixed the wing as best we can. Hopefully, that will be enough to please her," said Troy.

Josh nodded. "Let us hope so. I don't want another war like we had with the Black Dragon. Give the red dragon back her infant." Quietly, he dropped his weapons to the ground, but the sudden movement startled the dragon, and she started to rear.

Troy called out, "Here is your infant. Take him and go. We mean you no harm." She continued to rise. The children screamed as they ran to their parents.

A loud roar, and more dragons arrived. *They must have been nearby,* Josh thought. He heard a familiar bark. "Warrior, where have you been?" Everyone looked intently at the dog as he sat with the dragons.

"You will not hurt these people, Mystique," spoke an albino dragon. The red dragon obeyed and took her child.

The villagers bowed out of reverence and fear. "You can speak," said Josh. "The stories we heard from our grandfathers, they are true."

"Yes. Many years ago, peace was brought between all the mountain clans and us. It has remained that way with a promise to help protect you and them from your enemies, until something happened to Kannisdid, the one you call the Black Dragon. That is when the terror for all the villages and us started," said the albino dragon. "You are the warriors who fought the one you call the Black Dragon."

"We are," answered Josh as he eyed the creature. "My dog seems to know you."

"He and I are friends. I wish to thank you and your people for what you did. Kannisdid was our king. Now he can no longer rule over us, and we are free from his tyranny. Your village along with the others have been guarded by us from invaders for many years, and we will continue to do so. If you need us, send Warrior."

"The Black Dragon is dead then?" asked Troy.

Another dragon spoke, "No, he is not dead. He had two hearts. For him, to damage one was only to cripple him, not to kill him. But you left him, so he cannot fly. He lives in his lair and catches what he can. He is attracting followers though. So we watch him closely."

"Is killing him is out of the question?" asked Troy.

"As much as it would solve many problems, he was our king, and we will not slay him. We hoped he would die or be killed in battle," said the albino dragon. "You did your best."

"Thank you for protecting us all these years," said Josh. "What is your name?"

"My name is Ligia. We will go now." She looked at Warrior. "Goodbye, my friend. Take care of these people.

People watched the dragons leave. They did not understand what they had just witnessed. "Josh, you have any idea what those dragons were talking about?" asked Carl.

"Not sure, but if I remember the stories from my grandfather, they used to be friends with a dragon, and he was their protector from the king of the land. It would stop the king from sending his army to take taxes, slaves, and whatever else he wanted. I don't know how true any of it is."

"Looks like some of it is, my friend," said Troy.

Chapter 3

Josh dragged the filthy trunk into the inn and looked around. The place was empty.

Harmon, the innkeeper, came hobbling out from the backroom with a keg of ale. "You look like you've been digging in the mud. Bit late to be planting or harvesting, so you must have been exploring."

"Harmon, what makes you think I wasn't hunting?" asked Josh as he walked toward the bar.

"Well," explained Harmon as he placed the keg of ale on the counter, "you were in here last week, saying how you were done hunting for the season, and then there's that chest."

"So there is." Josh laughed. "Help me bring it over?"

The two men struggled to carry the heavy trunk alongside the wall beside a table.

"How did you manage to get this beast here?"

"It wasn't easy. You have some rags, so we can clean this up?"

"Yeah. You know where everything is. Need to rest my leg a bit after carrying that."

"No problem." Josh got the pail of water, and they started wiping off the caked-on mud and dirt.

Some of the village men drifted in and gawked at Josh and Harmon. "Besides making a mess, and keeping our innkeeper from serving us, what are you doing, Joshua?" asked Carl.

"Explored a cave and found this. Saw the initials and decided to bring it here."

"Whose initials?" asked Troy, the village doctor, as the rest of the men gathered around the table.

"JKL—Joshua Kendrick Lendremburger. My father, grandfather, or great-grandfather." Josh laughed. The rest of the men laughed with him. Everyone knew in that family the eldest son continued the family name. Josh had broken that rule by not naming his son Joshua but Reuben. But then Josh did a lot of things differently from his father and grandfather.

"I am surprised anything survived from your father's home. It was one of the first places to be completely destroyed by the dragons," said Carl.

"Yeah, I know," said Joshua as he brushed off the dust and looked at the lock. It was old and rusty. He took out his knife to see if he could break it when Carl's ax swung down on it and broke it open.

"Thanks." He lifted the lid. The chest was full of hardbound books. These were old and, from the look of them, were ones like his father, grandfather, and great-grandfather would have made. Joshua carefully picked up one.

"Look," yelled Troy. "The book underneath." On the cover was a young man riding a dragon, and the title read <u>Ligia.</u>

Josh was about to pick up the book when Warrior, his dog, dashed in. He stopped, barked, and turned toward the door, wanting Josh to follow him.

"Okay, boy, I'm coming." Followed by the rest of the men, they crossed the river and headed south. An hour later, they came to a field where Ligia, the queen, and a dozen other dragons waited. A green dragon they had met before needed help.

"Let's see if we can help him, Ligia," said Josh.

After a quick examination, Troy said, "He is in bad shape. The things I need are at the village."

"Mystique, give Troy a ride to the village," commanded Ligia to a red dragon. "Hang on tight to her neck, Troy, and you will be fine."

Troy took a deep breath and climbed on. As soon as he clutched Mystique's neck, they were airborne.

A deep voice asked, "Can you save my friend, Zurvan?"

Josh stopped and observed the massive creature sitting on a pile of rocks.

"This is my son, King Zurrum," said Ligia.

"We will do everything we can," said Josh. He could not believe the size of Zurrum. He dwarfed everything around him, just like his father. And he was black with the same crown of spikes. Zurrum had the same wicked spikes on his tail that was constantly moving. The only difference was he had a white stripe down his chest.

As much as Josh and his men wanted to scrutinize Zurrum, they needed to focus on the wounded dragon. "We need water to slow the bleeding."

Zurvan had a deep diagonal gash across his chest. One of the men splashed water across the dragon's face and then gave him some to drink. As they watched, his labored breathing lessened.

"Perhaps a little more," said Zurrum.

Josh nodded. The wounded dragon's breathing eased a bit more.

"They are returning," said Ligia.

Troy jumped off Mystique, holding two buckets, two books, and medicine. "I have everything needed to help your friend. Just need a fire."

"We gave him some water. And I will get a fire going," said Josh.

"Good." A few hours later and after consulting the books he had found in the chest, Troy finished closing all the wounds on Zurvan.

"Zurrum—need to talk," whispered Zurvan.

"You need to rest, my friend," answered Zurrum.

"No, this can't wait. Your father has many dragons in the Valley of Clouds."

"You are sure?" asked Zurrum.

"Followed Ligia's sister. She met with him. Needed to know how many dragons were there. I flew lower and many nests, so many. Was attacked."

"Rest now, Zurvan."

They all looked at one another, deep in their own thoughts.

"Zurrum, you are king now. Does that mean you will fight Kannisdid?" asked Josh.

"I will see if he will agree to my terms and stay with his dragons in the Valley of Clouds. If not, then there will be war. We need to protect your people and mine."

It was with relief that Josh and the rest of the men heard this news as they watched Zurrum, Ligia, and some of the other dragons leave. At least not having to fight that beast alone was a comfort especially after their last encounter. But to know he had built up a sizable army was disconcerting.

Chapter 4

Zurrum, Ligia, and many Guardians of the Throne dragons arrived at the Valley of Clouds.

The sun hung low in the sky, giving way to pink streaks as a silver mist and pungent smell rose from the ground.

Zurrum looked at one of the dragons and nodded. The dragon flew higher into the sky. The dragons flew underneath the cloud cover.

Kannisdid or the Black Dragon and Ethelinda, Ligia's sister, sat on a flat ledge on the mountain and feigned surprise at their coming. Zurrum knew they were not as their coming was not a secret. They landed near to where he and his followers were.

Zurrum looked at the scars and limp wing. Despite these injuries, Kannisdid still had a commanding presence.

"What do you want, Zurrum? You, the self-proclaimed king of the dragons, I suppose I should show you some respect," he said sarcastically.

"I expect none. I came to give you an ultimatum. You and your dragons stay in the Valley of Clouds or face the consequences."

"Give me a day to think about it," said Kannisdid as he shuffled toward Zurrum.

"No," Zurrum replied firmly, not backing up. "Give the answer now."

"Here is my answer. I do as I please," he bellowed as twenty more of his dragons joined him on the mountain.

Suddenly, the air was filled with flames as the Guardians lit the air around Kannisdid.

Zurrum signaled for them to halt. "Do you really think I would come alone? That we trust you?"

"We hoped, and we waited for you to come to us in peace, but it was in vain. You are evil, and your hatred for mankind has made you our enemy. Your name meant gentle heart, but your name has been changed to Neimacreorth or the evil one."

Neimacreorth wanted to fight. It showed in his eyes, but he knew better. His time would come. The Guardians of the Throne were dangerous, and not knowing how many there were, he would wait.

Zurrum continued, "It was written many years ago that we would protect these mountain people. It was an oath taken between us and man. You have broken that sacred trust."

The clouds were starting to roll back in. Soon it would be difficult to see anything.

Zurrum raised his head and roared out so all could hear him. "This is my only warning to you and your followers. Heed me well! If you leave the Valley of Clouds, you will die. That includes you, Ethelinda. No longer are you safe outside these mountains."

With that, Zurrum and the dragons left, and the valley was enshrouded with clouds.

Chapter 5

Josh and his men were assembled by the river with all their weapons, along with the traps, bows, and arrows they had made. Until they heard back from Zurrum, they would prepare for war. Everyone else in the village had gone underground or into the caves, taking their livestock and crops with them. It was a temporary solution at best.

Sentries had been posted farther from town, but even that would not be enough if Kannisdid sent his army.

Zurrum landed close to Josh. "We prepare to go to war."

Josh stared at Zurrum. "I wish I could say I was surprised but—"

"There is more," stated Zurrum, "Neimacreorth as he is now called can fly!"

Josh could feel himself turning pale. He looked at the ashen men beside him. "Are you sure?" he choked out.

"There is only one way to get onto the plateau he was on, and that is to fly. Also, his army is large. We must defend you here as well as protect our own home."

"This time, you will not fight alone," promised Zurrum. "Dragons! Get to know your warrior. Carry him into battle when it is time. Trust one another. Only by trusting one another will we be able to defeat such a formidable foe as Neimacreorth and his forces."

One day turned into two, then three, still no sign of Neimacreorth. What was he waiting for? Time? They were able to make more weapons. With Zurrum's help and going through the books, they made saddles for the dragons to carry men with weapons.

They practiced flying at different speeds and angles and then using weapons. Josh did not understand Neimacreorth. "Why wait? Was he wanting a fair fight?"

"No," answered a voice behind him. "I'm sure that is one thing he is not wanting." Josh had been so caught up with his own thoughts he had not realized he was talking aloud and had not heard Troy come up behind him.

"That beast is up to something." Troy winced as he tried to get the kinks out of his neck and back after spending another sleepless night with a sick child. "Maybe it has to do with the age of his dragons and the weather."

"Winter is almost upon us. You would think it wouldn't be a good time for an attack," said Josh.

"Perhaps not, but if they catch us off guard and in deep snow . . ." speculated Troy.

"Very true," agreed Josh.

"So we wait."

"We wait."

Thick clouds had rolled in the early evening and with it a bitter wind and the first snowstorm. By late afternoon, the storm had moved on after dumping more than three feet of snow.

Josh bundled up and took the dogs and went to check on the widows and elderly. This was something he set up when he became chief. Everyone was responsible to help someone else, whether it was to the tunnels or to the caves across the bridge. They could not afford to lose any more people.

After checking the village, he took the dogs for a run in the field. The sun was just starting to set. Warrior left. Boomer growled!

Josh stared. A small light, in the distance, grew larger and brighter by the second. What was that? The light was blinding! Josh had to shield his eyes and hope he could see it. As the light approached, he could make out a faint outline, but nothing else.

Soon the light gave way to a wizened-looking snout-faced dragon. The large owllike eyes saw everything but saw nothing. The creature tilted his red-crested bearded head and folded back his rainbow wings, which exposed his red crystalline chest.

Josh stood, transfixed! Never had he seen anything like this. A crystal dragon!

"My name is Valgus. Are you chief of this village?" he asked politely.

"Yes," stammered Josh.

Like magic, Carl was beside him with a dragon he had not seen before. This one had feathers like an eagle all over its body.

Those feathers would make a warm quilt or bed, thought Josh.

Heard that, came a response.

"Who said that?" asked Josh.

"I will explain later," said Carl, "but this dragon can read your mind and talks to you the same way."

"Ah, my friend, it has been a long time," said Valgus. "Of course, I would not be here if it wasn't important. What was that? Am I going to take Neimacreorth's side? No. No. No. You don't understand. He sent many messengers to find me, and well, you know, deliver the messages, or fight Neimacreorth. I have just come to deliver a message to the person in charge and to the king of the dragons. Yes, I know it is too late to deliver to the king as they have left or are in hibernation, but you will do it for me. Thank you so much. Oh, the message!

"I, Valgus was once your king and left because of a human who needed my help. Neimacreorth became king. Man betrayed him. But he should still be king because he did not give up his right to rule the dragons. So by dawn of spring, that right will be returned to him, or all followers of Zurrum will be slain." Valgus looked away from the Winter Dragon and spoke to Josh and Carl.

"To the village people, you have until the dawn of spring to leave these mountains or die."

Josh and Carl looked at each other and then the dragons. "So nothing's changed then," said Carl.

"No, we just have an ultimatum from the other side," said Josh.

"Take care of yourself and these people," said Valgus as he spread his wings and lit the area around him. He then rose effortlessly into the sky.

Winter Dragon shielded them from the light with his wing. He looked at Josh and shook his small craggy head. *I don't see how a dragon could be interested in eating something as skinny as a human. Now a dog, now that . . .*

Josh heard the thoughts and shook his head, trying to get rid of them. "Remember what I said. This is how this creature talks to you, "reminded Carl.

"My dog, Warrior, is best friend's with Ligia, queen of the dragons, and Boomer is my other dog. Leave them alone."

Oh!

"Yes, oh. There is plenty of wild game around," said Josh.

I am protecting you, so maybe you would be willing to share some moose with me. One of my favorites.

"Where you came from, when you wanted to eat something, what did you do?" asked Josh.

I would go to the river and sit on the highest rock and wait.

20

It was strange having someone else's thoughts running through your mind, but he would try and get used to it. Josh looked at Winter Dragon and pointed toward the river. "There's the river. Help yourself."

The dragon muttered something unintelligently. *I am sure you could do nicely with just one dog.*

"I heard that," called out Josh. "What kind of dragon is Valgus? *You would call it a blinder dragon.*

Chapter 6

Josh and Carl along with the two dogs trudged through the snow to the inn, discussing the two dragons. When they reached the inn, Carl explained to everyone there about Winter Dragon, while Josh emphasized they keep a careful watch on their dogs and about the message delivered by Valgus. There was a smattering of laughter, but they all agreed to keep a watch on the few dogs left.

"What about this other dragon?" asked one of the men.

"I don't know," Josh said. "Has Troy brought any of the books back?"

"No, can't say as I've seen him for some time," said the innkeeper.

"I know he's reading up on the different types of dragons. Maybe he has read something about Valgus and our so-called winter protection," said Josh. "I'll see what he's found out. It looks like it will be a long, frigid winter. Make sure everyone has enough food and wood and keep working on your weapons."

Troy lived outside the village. He preferred to be by himself especially when he worked on his medicines. Troy used different herbs, flowers, and trees to make them, some of which smelled like rotting flesh or worse.

As Josh approached Troy's large two-level home, he noticed there was no smoke coming from the chimney. Warrior had come with him and barked as they neared the house. Josh sunk up to knee-deep snow before he was able to find the wooden path again. Warrior ran ahead, scratched at the door, looked back at Josh, and waited for the door to open. Nothing happened. Finally, Josh reached the door and pounded on it.

"Troy, open the door. Are you all right?' He heard a slight sound and pounded on the door again. This time, a crash from inside. Josh grabbed a stool that was beside the door and dragged it over to the window. Balanced on it, he pulled out his knife and managed to get it between the shutters and lift the bar holding them in place. He sheathed his knife and broke the shutter, and the stench almost knocked him backward off the stool. It smelled like rotten flesh! Warrior jumped past him. Josh took a deep breath of cold air and climbed in. The dim light cast a shadow on the wall where a cloaked figure leaned.

Josh ran to the door, threw it open, and took a deep breath. Then he went back to get the clad figure and Warrior, who struggled for air. Josh threw the figure over his shoulder and laid him out in the snow and ran back in, picked up Warrior, and laid him beside an ashen Troy.

The strange odor started to dissipate, though now it seemed vaguely familiar. Josh shook Troy sat him up and hoped to get some response. A groan escaped Troy's lips. He would be okay! Warrior was up and sat beside them. "Troy, what happened?"

"Worked on medicine. Didn't work out."

"I can see that. I'm going to start a fire. Come on. It smells better inside now."

"Let me sit here. Go ahead." Troy bent his head into his knees and pulled his cloak up close around him.

Josh looked back at the dark figure, very worried, and hurried inside to start a fire. When he came back ten minutes later, Troy still had not moved. "Come, my friend. I have put on water to boil and bread to eat. You will feel better soon." Lifting Troy up, Josh helped him inside to the table where he slouched into a chair and sighed but refused to take off his oversized cloak.

Josh went to help him take off the cloak, but Troy pushed him away.

"No! Not now. I will take it off when I am ready."

"All right, here drink this and try and eat something. Then you should lie down and get some rest," Josh said as he patted Warrior.

Soon Troy went upstairs to lie down but still refused to take off his cloak. Joshua did not push the issue; he would use the time to look over the books on the dragons.

He found the trunk and took the books out, hoping to find a book on blinder dragons. The shadows were long in the house when he lit a lantern and pulled out the last of the books. Nothing!

Josh picked up a particularly heavy book to put back in the trunk when the bottom moved. Could it be? He carefully lifted the book out and pushed on the left side of the trunk. Nothing happened. He moved his hand along the inside edge of the trunk. There it was, a faint click. Josh pushed on the back of the trunk and then the front. Suddenly, the bottom swung up, revealing a false bottom.

Josh grinned. There were two cloths covering something. It was difficult to get them out. By using his knife, he pried them up and lifted the cloth-covered objects out. Josh uncovered one and then the other. Both were medium-sized slender boxes with a keyhole lock for one and combination lock for the other.

"The key and combination must be here somewhere." Josh started to feel inside the trunk again. A shadow fell across the trunk.

"What are you looking for?" asked the cloaked figure gruffly.

Joshua leaned back against the trunk, looked up, and hoped to see Troy. "You scared me, my . . . Troy, is that you?" Josh wasn't sure what he was seeing. Should he run, scream? The very hairs on his neck stood on end. Troy's usually robust face had become ashen, with sunken catlike eyes, and hollow cheeks. His voice was deeper, threatening, not the gentle person he knew.

"Leave this place, now!"

"No, not until you tell me what is wrong with you. It has nothing to do with experiments either." He reached for his friend.

"Don't touch me. I told you to leave this place. The boxes. You found the boxes. Give them to me," Troy demanded as he sunk to his knees. A key dangled from his neck.

"No, not until—"

A wicked backhand sent Josh flailing backward into the wall. The door was thrown open, and Carl and Warrior rushed in. Carl ran to grab Troy. Warrior jumped at him from the side and knocked him over and stood beside Troy, snarling and growling, daring either one to come any closer.

"Are you okay?" asked Carl and Josh together. Both nodded. "Do you have any idea what is going on here?" asked Carl. "I mean, for your dog to turn against us and Troy to do what he did. Saw it through the window."

Josh rubbed his chin and took a good look at Warrior and then Troy. "It has something to do with those boxes. And whatever had happened to Troy."

Chapter 7

Troy pulled the key from around his neck and motioned for Josh to hand him the box. It was too late. Troy passed out. Warrior whined and pawed at him, but he did not move.

"Open the box," said a voice behind them." Carl and Josh turned and saw Valgus at the open door. "Hurry, do as I say, or he will not live through the night."

Carl grabbed the key from Troy's hand. Josh placed the slender pine box on the table. Carl opened the box. Both men were stunned! What they saw left them speechless.

"Put the ruby dragon in Troy's hand and bring him to me," directed Valgus.

Josh took the ruby dragon and placed it in Troy's outstretched hand. He immediately clutched it tightly. They lifted Troy and brought him to Valgus.

"Do not let anyone have those boxes. Guard them with your lives. We will return tomorrow." With that, Valgus grasped Troy in his claws and disappeared into the night sky.

"Another threat, I think. Anyway, your family was wondering where you were. That's why I came," Carl said. "Do you have any idea what is going on?"

"No! Yes! Sort of. What are we supposed to do with these boxes? Protect with our lives. Right. Look at this: three more dragons—one jade, one diamond, and one onyx. Must be worth a fortune. Makes you wonder what's in the other box."

"Not really. Had enough surprises. What are we going to do about the boxes? You heard Valgus."

Josh closed the lid and locked the pine box, while he thought about what to do. "Let's just put them back where I found them for now and say nothing to anyone about what happened here tonight."

"Sounds good to me. Now you say you understand what is going on. Could you please explain it to me?" asked Carl as he handed more books to Josh to put away in the trunk.

"Well, as I understand it, the dragons and people were at war. Then dragons had riders and were at war with different kingdoms. Somewhere along the line, it was dragon versus man again. Then something happened here in the high country where there was peace between the two. Something happened to Neimacreorth, which brought war on people again. Now it's dragons against dragons and people. Got it."

"Of course. Any idea where Troy, Valgus, and the mystery boxes fit in?"

"No idea! But tomorrow is a new day." He gave his friend a slap on the back. "So I am off home before they think I am dead. And you, my friend?"

"I will wait here."

In the early morning, Josh made his way back to Troy's house. First, he checked on some families, and the dogs had a good run in the field. On the horizon, he watched as dark, heavy clouds hovered above the mountains. Before going to Troy's, he stopped at the inn to see how Harmon was doing. Sure enough, the door was open, and the large stone fireplace still had warm embers. Josh grabbed a few sticks and blew lightly on the embers until they caught fire. Then he added more dry kindling. Soon he had a large fire going. Harmon came in.

"Thank you, Josh. Have you talked to Troy yet?" he asked as he limped over to the chair by the fireplace.

"Yes. If anyone comes in, tell them it looks like this storm could last two to three days. They need to clear paths as much as possible and string ropes between houses and barns. Make sure the animals are well-fed. You have enough wood?"

"Yes."

"Okay! I will see you in a few days." With that, Josh pulled on his deerskin gloves and left the tavern.

Outside, Josh felt the wind picking up. Soon the storm would hit. "Boomer home. I'll be there soon, at least I hope so," he whispered to himself.

As he plowed through the snow with Warrior beside him, he soon came to the wooden path to Troy's home. It was completely clear.

"Carl must have . . ."

He did not. I did. I will have you know.

"Not you," Josh said as he glared at Winter Dragon.

Of course, me.

"When are you leaving?"

When your beautiful winter season is done.

A groan escaped Josh's lips as he walked into the house. Carl was slumped over the kitchen table, fast asleep. He had been reading a book and lay with his face buried in it. Josh shook his head and laughed.

The fire was out, so Josh strode to the stone hearth, took the poker, and poked the half-burned log to see if it would flare up again. A few sparks flew off it. Josh blew on it and added some paper and twigs. Soon a small fire started. He added a larger log and then put water on to boil.

Warrior had gone over to Carl and stood on his hind legs and nuzzled his arm. All he got was a grunt in response. Warrior did what he always did, tugged at Carl's sleeve, and when that did not work, he licked his face.

"What was that?" yelled Carl as he jerked wide awake.

"Well, you wouldn't wake up." Josh laughed. Warrior barked and wagged his tail.

"Thanks a lot."

The door opened with a blast of frigid air and swirling snow. A clad figure walked in with staff in hand. "Thanks for clearing my pathway," said Troy as he closed the door and pulled off his cloak.

Carl and Josh rushed to his side. "You're all right?" asked Josh.

"Of course. Why wouldn't I be?"

Both men looked at the healthy man standing before them. His strength had returned. He had color in his face and a sparkle in his green eyes. Even his black hair had a sheen to it.

"What happened last night?" asked Josh.

"You need to go. The storm is getting worse. It will probably last two or three days."

Carl looked out the window. "He is right. It has moved in fast."

"We will go, Troy, but when this storm is over, I will be back, and you will tell me everything. Understood?"

Troy gave a slight nod.

They stepped outside to a snow-laden path and a ferocious wind. They bent into the howling wind and watched as the wind whipped the trees around. Broken branches tossed unto houses and barns like a tornado, dropping everything in its wake. Soon the snow would blind them. They needed to hurry.

Carl managed to plow toward his home. While Josh and Warrior continued, he paused and listened. Was that a gate banging? The falling trees and branches along with the wind made it difficult to tell where the noise came from. A nudge at his side. "Okay, Warrior, I'm coming. Open gates, mean loose animals, and sure death in this storm."

As he got closer, he thought he heard a child's voice. Warrior barked. A child struggled to get all the goats into the shed. Warrior herded the frightened animals into the shed, while Josh clutched up the child, bent into the wind, grabbed the safety rope, and delivered her to her home.

He followed the rope back to the shed, went inside, and made sure the animals were safe. Then he grabbed some rope for a collar for Warrior, stepped outside, made sure the shed was locked, and then shut and bolted the gate. Warrior barked. Josh could just make out his outline. The dog's multicolor coat became a layer of frozen snow as he struggled through it. "Coming." Josh managed to reach Warrior, but they were off the wooden walkway. The snow deepened with each passing minute and, without his snowshoes, became more difficult. Hopefully, they were going in the right direction. He could not even see the village anymore. "I should let Neimacreorth have this land and move to someplace warmer? What do you think my friend?" He gasped. Warrior barked. "I thought so."

"Keep moving, boy." He clutched Warrior's collar in his gloved hand. "Ow! My foot." Warrior whined. "The walkway. Now which way to go." Keeping one hand on Warrior, with the other, he dug away snow until he could at least feel the walkway.

"Any ideas, Warrior?" as he helped the dog onto the path. So tired from the cold and snow, he could not get his bearings. Josh leaned down beside his faithful friend and listened. He heard him sniff the wood and air. Warrior barked.

"All right, if this is the direction you say, then I'll start plodding through." It was difficult going. Warrior sunk in the soft snow, so Josh had to keep one hand on him while making tracks. He needed to keep his balance, which at times was not easy with the velocity of the wind. A broken branch served as a staff. It helped with his balance and kept them on the path.

Exhaustion started to settle in. Josh knew he had to keep them moving, or they would freeze to death. "Was that a bark?" Josh shivered. Warrior barked. Another dog answered. "Boomer, yes, it's Boomer. Almost home." A renewed surge of energy hit them both, and they plowed through the snow toward Boomer's barking. Then he saw a faint light in a window.

"Go toward the light, Warrior. That's it." Josh lost sight of it. Then he saw it again as his head banged against the overhang supports of his home.

A door swung open, and Josh fell inside, and Warrior crawled in on top of him.

Chapter 8

In the morning, Josh woke to the sound of the wind whistling and howling through the trees. His two children were snuggled in bed with him. His wife, Helena, was stirring stew at the fireplace.

A sudden blast and roar-like thunder shook the house. Pots rattled and swung on racks. Dishes clattered onto the wooden floor. Both children screamed. "Shush, children. It is only the wind," said Helena reassuringly.

Another blast of icy cold wind blew through the cracks of the house. Helena clutched their daughter tightly. Nine-year-old Reuben grabbed his knife. Both dogs growled and snarled at something outside.

Something else is going on outside, thought Josh as he listened intently to the bangs and crashes of the trees falling around them. "Into the cellar! We will wait out the storm there."

Two days later, the storm stopped. The four of them were relieved to get out of the cellar. "What happened? Our dishes and clothes are strewn everywhere?" Josh stood and looked at the mess in disbelief. "Everything is wet."

"How did we get a hole in the roof?" asked Helena as she helped her daughter out of the cellar.

"It couldn't have been," answered Josh. "Was there really a fight, or was I imagining it?"

"The dogs are eating the stew you made, Ma." A cheerful Emilia laughed as she sat down beside the dogs and petted them. "They're helping clean up the mess."

"Rueben and I will go outside and check the house. Then dig our way to the animals." Boomer and Warrior were right behind them. Both dogs barked.

At first, Josh did not see anything when he scanned the area. "What is that? Looks like an animal trapped in tree branches."

Help me.

"Winter Dragon?"

Yes! Hurry.

"Coming as fast as I can." Josh searched for his snowshoes. He and Reuben dug them out and set out to help the dragon. "Rueben, sound the alarm, then tend to our animals." Josh heard the ram's horn sound twice. Then someone answered in return. *Help is coming.* He trudged through the snow, threw branches out of the way, and sidestepped others. He could hear the dogs panting behind him. Josh glanced back and saw three men headed in his direction.

Hurry! There is little time!

"What happened? You look like you have been caged in branches." He tried to walk around the dragon but was stopped short.

I will explain later. Cut the branches in front and the one that has pierced the front of my wing.

Josh was already removing what branches he could with his hands. Then he pulled out his knife and cut away at the branches close to the wing. By then, the other men arrived. "Help me get this piece of branch that has pierced his wing, Carl. You other two keep clearing away the branches and check around his back and make sure the tree hasn't fallen or blocked him in any way."

As soon as the branch was removed from his wing, Winter Dragon flapped his wings and flew off. He left a trail of crimson blood in the white snow. The men stood there dumbfounded, unsure as to what had just happened.

All at once, a bloodcurdling shriek and deafening roar shook the skies overhead. Terrified, the men jumped back into the safety of the trees. They gripped the dogs as both snarled and barked at the noise. Screams came from the village.

Blood flowed from the sky like rain. Winter Dragon had landed on top of another dragon, who looked to be golden in color. He had his talons firmly grasped into its body and attempted to get a firm grip on the dragon's neck. The golden dragon tried to flip Winter Dragon off by rolling in midair. Its neck was twisted backward. He tried to evade, bite, and spit fire at Winter Dragon all at the same time. It was a horrible spectacle. But mesmerizing. The two dragons rolled four times and then hit the ground. Neither one seemed dazed by it.

Then the fiery duel began. They faced each other and circled; each tried to get an advantage. Both dragons evaded the other's fiery blast, so no damage was done other than blood flowed down from both and pooled on the melted crimson snow. Soon both exhausted their fire, and the golden dragon tried to flee. Winter Dragon launched a vicious attack again. He drove the dragon up and grabbed its neck with its talons. Then with all the force he had left, he drove it down onto the roof of Josh's house. The golden dragon lay stunned. Winter Dragon picked it up and dropped it on the ground. He let out an earth-shattering roar, landed on the beast, and killed it. Then he picked up the dead carcass and carried it off.

The men were stunned by what they had witnessed. "Where did that dragon come from?" asked one of the men.

"Don't know," replied Josh.

An angry roar and beating wings were heard overhead. Winter Dragon landed a short distance from them. Blood flowed from scratches and a gash along its side.

"Let us help you," implored Josh.

Of course. There were two dragons. I am sure Neimacreorth sent them to spy on the village and see if Valgus was here. The wolvers will dispose of their bodies.

"Thank you! My wife can tend to your wounds," Josh said.

Winter Dragon flew to the house where Helena waited outside with her daughter. She disappeared inside and came out with sewing materials and medicine for the dragon's wounds. Within an hour, Winter Dragon was patched up and calmed down.

Josh and Carl took stock of the house, and the other two men continued clearing paths to their homes. "Move your family to the inn?" asked Carl.

"Good idea," agreed Josh. "It will be a couple of days before we get this repaired."

Three days later, the roof was fixed, and Winter Dragon stood guard. Now it was time to see what happened to Troy.

Chapter 9

Gray skies did not help Josh's mood as he trudged along the wooden path toward Troy's home. "Yes, another storm was coming. No, I'm not sure about dragons and why they were here. Valgus, perhaps? People wanted answers. I have no answers! We should have nothing to worry about except snow and wild animals. Now we have these beasts back in our lives. Is this good or not? I don't know."

Josh pounded on Troy's door and yelled, "Open up!" A surprised Troy stood at the door. "I want the truth, now." He pushed past his friend and sat down. Warrior followed. Josh looked sternly at him "You be quiet or go home." Warrior growled!

"Just because you are angry doesn't mean you have to take it out on your dog."

"You're right. I'm sorry, Warrior." He leaned over and placed his head on top of his dog's. Josh sat up and sighed as he petted his faithful friend. "Tell me what happened to you."

"Valgus and I hoped no one would ever find out." Josh said nothing. "I found Valgus's lair while exploring the mountains. We became friends. I found a dragon egg and had to get it to him before anyone else found it. So under cover of night, I took the egg to the lair. It was storming. Before continuing the climb, I stopped to rest at the base of an old cedar tree.

When I woke, I was in the lair. Valgus told me lightning struck me, the tree, and the egg. I should have died, but instead I can change into—"

"A dragon," a voice said behind them. Both men looked up to see Carl standing in the doorway.

"Yes. Come and sit."

"What do the jewels have to do with it? And the dragon egg?" asked Josh.

"I am not really sure how to explain it myself. I found the boxes of gem dragons at the market, and they were in my bag." The two men exchanged knowing glances. "The whole cave lit up like shooting stars whenever I touched the walls with them."

Troy took the ruby dragon over to the fireplace. As soon as it warmed up, it glowed and sparked. "Went to work with a seer to learn to control the length of time I spent being a dragon. Valgus helped. But during the wars, we were separated. He got the rubies and hid them. As for the dragon, it did hatch, but what became of her, I don't know."

"You could have helped, and you didn't?" yelled Carl.

"No, Carl," replied Troy calmly. "I couldn't. That would mean telling the entire village so they would not kill me. Besides, if you watched closely, those dragons were fighting among themselves."

Both Carl and Josh looked at each other. Josh thought back to some fights he had seen Ligia in. "You are right. They were already fighting among themselves."

"The problem I have right now is the plants I need were destroyed, and some are rare. I have enough to get me through the winter. I hope this spring gives me the plants I need," said Troy.

"So what do we do?" asked Josh. "Do we tell the rest of the council members?"

"No, we keep it to ourselves. You are our chief, and I am on the council. It's good enough," said Carl.

"Is there anything else we can help you with?" asked Josh. Troy shook his head as he replaced the ruby around his neck. "All right, we shall go."

Once outside, Warrior ran ahead, and the men walked on in silence. Josh looked at the threatening storm clouds, glad his roof was repaired.

Carl broke the silence. "People would not understand how he did nothing and let innocent people die."

Chapter 10

Another storm! This winter is colder, harder on everyone, he thought as he stood in the doorway and watched the snow come swirling down. Josh knew what Carl said was true. *The people would not understand about Troy being a dragon, but he fought alongside them and helped them whenever he could. If it did come out about him being a dragon, I could only hope people remember what he has done for them.*

A loud crash-like thunder brought his wife to his side. "What is it?" asked Helena.

"I can't tell till this storm dies down," said a worried Josh. "Hopefully, Winter Dragon is all right." Josh knew from the roar Winter Dragon had attacked something. Later that evening, the storm subsided. Josh went to find the dragon.

"Winter Dragon, what happened to you? You have fresh wounds."

The dragon is dead. I will be fine. Troy took care of me.

"Are these dragons being sent by Neimacreorth?"

Yes. He would not let another group of dragons move into his territory unless he gave them his permission or wanted something from them. Only King Zurrum has the power to allow dragons to move from one territory to another. I will tell Zurrum as soon as I can.

"Thank you, Winter Dragon." Josh plowed through the snow, thinking of happier days, children's laughter, playing, not worrying about homes being destroyed or villages.

Josh opened the inn door. The fire crackled and popped as Harman, the bartender, stoked the log in the hearth. "Harman, I need to send messages to the other villages with your carrier pigeons. Need to find out whether they have been attacked too."

"No problem. You write it up. I'll get the birds ready."

Within a couple of hours, the birds were released. "They should all be back within the week. You look like you could use a drink. Come on," said Harman as he pushed Josh toward the bar.

A week later, all the birds were back, and the news was bad. Josh read the notes to the men assembled at the inn. "All the villages have been attacked. Have we missed something? Zurrum told Neimacreorth and his followers if they left the Valley of Clouds, they would be killed," Josh said thoughtfully.

"Maybe there is another way off the mountain Zurrum doesn't know about?" questioned Carl. "Those beasts would have had a lot of time to explore it."

Troy looked at everyone and spoke, "Why didn't I think of this before? Zurrum brought in dragons from other areas who could withstand our cold and therefore protect us. Why wouldn't Neimacreorth do the same thing?"

Josh left the inn angry with himself. He had not thought of something like that when talking with Winter Dragon. Perhaps when they talked again, they could figure out where they came from.

Winter Dragon landed close to the river. Josh saw him through the pines and headed in his direction. *I wonder where the dogs are. Haven't seen them all day.*

A sick feeling hit him in the pit of his stomach. Winter Dragon had been hurt. He wouldn't have . . . A bark from the river sent a sense of relief flooding through Josh as Boomer crawled out from behind a bush. He limped toward Josh; blood trickled down his face and legs.

"I need help!" yelled Josh as he ran toward Boomer. "Get Troy. I've got you, boy." Blood flowed from his side; the cold kept him from bleeding to death. "Anyone seen Warrior?"

"No!" came the unanimous reply.

"Where were you and dogs hurt, Winter Dragon?" asked Troy.

We battled in a cave on the far side of the mountain.

"Carl, help me take Boomer home. Everyone else, search for Warrior. If he's injured, he won't survive the night."

"Winter Dragon, these fights keep opening up old wounds," said Troy as blood seeped from more cuts. "It is weakening you."

It is not a problem. Fix me. I will look for Warrior.

Josh needed to concentrate on Boomer, but he was worried about Warrior. With the snow so deep, finding him would not be easy, especially if he lay unconscious somewhere. He knew the men would not give up either.

Troy checked Boomer. Looked like a fractured leg and a lot of cuts. Plus, some singed hair. He had a lump on his neck. "He will be okay once we set his leg and take care of all these cuts."

The last of the grim-faced men came in in the early morning. They searched along the river and forest with torches. There had been signs of a fight—trees knocked down, melted bloody snow, and burned brush, but that was all. Even Winter Dragon came back with a defeated look on his scarred face. Inside the house, Boomer rested, stared at the door, and waited for his friend. There was no sign of Warrior.

In the morning, Josh made sure everyone was all right, but a feeling of despair covered the village. He hiked to the hill and started to look for Warrior. Josh needed to know if his dog was dead or alive. More of the villagers searched across the river and in the forest. Nothing!

Days turned into weeks. Boomer healed, and so did Winter Dragon. He flew farther upstream and looked for Warrior—nothing. Josh was desperate. He needed to know if Warrior was alive. He sent out the carrier pigeons again to see if anyone in the other villages had seen him or had him. All responses came back—no!

Boomer stayed close to Josh, always looked toward the mountain. "Had Warrior tried to go for help?" asked Josh.

"He may have," replied Troy. "It will be spring soon. We are getting low on food, and we must be aware of Neimacreorth's return."

"Yes, I know, but once the snow is gone, I need to look for Warrior one more time. Need to know for sure," Josh said sadly.

"I know, my friend. We all miss him."

Spring came, and most of the snow melted except for under the trees or densely forested areas. Josh grabbed his backpack and weapons and trudged toward the cave where the battle had taken place with Winter Dragon and the dogs. Boomer followed close behind.

Winter Dragon flew overhead. *Where are you going?*

"Need to see if I can find any trace of Warrior, and I need some fresh game."

He was your friend, but I have looked all over that area and more. He is not there. Hopefully, someone found him, or he made it to the Dragon's Lair. If not, he is dead. Do not go much farther in your search. It is not safe. I must return to the village.

Josh watched Winter Dragon leave and climbed on for another hour through mud and grass before he fell to his knees, looked up into the heavens, and screamed, knowing Winter Dragon might be right. Tears flowed freely. Boomer nudged him, whined, and Josh grasped him tightly and buried his face in the dog's neck.

It was dusk when Josh arrived at the inn. The men gathered there waited for an explanation. "Sorry, I just had to take one last look," Josh said. "Tonight, we hold a wake for Warrior, our hope when we saw none." The men cheered as this would give all a chance to share their grief. Each one grabbed a cup of ale and started to share stories.

"He went with the hunting parties and led us to where the best places to shoot deer and moose were," said someone.

"It's a good thing, or you would have starved," someone else chimed in. Mugs clanged, and laughter abounded.

"Remember when Warrior helped the children learn to fish with their hands. Always an interesting adventure and a lot of fun to watch," said Carl.

"He would visit the widows and orphans with me and comfort them," said Josh. "But most importantly, he fought alongside us, whether it was against wild animals or dragons." A murmur of agreement could be heard. "So a toast to one of the bravest warriors to ever fight with us. May we never forget Warrior and what he has done for us."

"Hear! Hear!" Cups clanged together and a moment of silence as they remembered their fallen comrade.

"Tomorrow, we start preparations for a new planting season, but also for a war with Neimacreorth," said Josh.

"I will come around to find out how many weapons everyone has, and we will decide how we can plow, fish, and hunt without Neimacreorth's followers finding out where we are," said Troy.

The men agreed, and each headed home. "The tunnels and caves will have to be checked," said Carl.

"The river overflowed, so we will have to be vigilant," said Josh. "I trust you to gather a couple of men to check the tunnels and caves in the next couple of days."

"It will be done. Have a good night."

Early the next morning, Josh visited the widows with Boomer. It seemed strange to do this without Warrior., but it had been three months, and people liked Boomer too. Young boys cut and stacked wood. If the widows needed help with household chores, the older girls helped, sometimes with younger siblings.

By midmorning, Josh walked over to the inn. He met with Troy, Carl, and Harmon. "We don't have enough weights for the nets we have made," said Troy. "A couple of men are molding more. Everyone is still making more spears and arrows."

"I have walked through the tunnels and set some men shoring up places that have been weakened by the snow and battles," said Carl. "I need to cut more wood for them."

"It sounds good. What have you heard, Harmon?" asked Josh.

"Everything is quiet, just like here. No reports of dragons, no battles, nothing. Very strange."

"You are right, Harmon. It is very strange." Boomer barked. All three men grabbed their weapons and ran to the door.

Boomer barked and ran toward the hill through the long dry grass. There were familiar barks in return. The grass moved, but nothing could be seen. "Warrior, could it be?"

"Is it Warrior?"

"I know that bark!"

Everyone talked at once. They waited and hoped, and sure enough, Boomer and Warrior greeted each other in the open field.

Josh found his voice, "Warrior," and ran toward his friend. Soon all the villagers surrounded the trio as Josh clutched Warrior in his arms.

"Tonight, we celebrate, for our friend has returned," shouted Josh. Everyone shouted and chanted Warrior's name. They were oblivious to the many scars on him or how he survived, only that he was home.

Keen eyes watched from the mountaintop.

Chapter 11

Josh opened the door to the sun already above the mountains. Carl strolled up the path. "Quite the celebration last night."

"Yes, one we all needed." Josh watched the men plowing in the field. "Something is wrong."

"The animals seem fine. Don't see anything out of order." Someone slapped them on their shoulders.

"Troy!" exclaimed Josh as they both spun around.

"Anyone seen Winter Dragon? He didn't look too good yesterday, so I need to check him over."

"No, but he may be down at the river having something to eat," said Carl.

"Let me grab my weapons, and we will check," replied Josh as he stepped back inside and grabbed his spear and bow and arrows.

The three men strolled through the grass while the dogs nipped at the heels of some goats being herded to the river. The children called for Warrior and Boomer for help, while men and women called out greetings to the chief and two elders.

Josh looked at the dragon's favorite hunting rock. "Where is he?"

"He should be here." Troy looked downstream but saw nothing.

"You see anything around the mountain or farther upstream, Carl?" Joshua was worried. The dogs had not growled or showed signs of anything being wrong. "Winter Dragon did say he could only stay as long as our winters. I wonder if he left or is at the snow line until Zurrum comes."

"I don't see anything, but he may be back tonight when it is colder. He will not be able to stay much longer. I would think Zurrum will be here soon along with other."

"There is Winter Dragon." Troy pointed to a large shadow coming from behind the mountain followed by two other similar shapes.

The three dragons landed close to the men, scattering the goats. *Sorry, my friends. It is time for me to leave. I have spoken to Zurrum. He should be here soon. Take care of yourselves.*

"Thank you for your care this past winter." Josh looked at their worn-out friend. His wings hung limp. He had so many injuries. His eyes betrayed the pain he felt. "Without you, I don't think we would have survived."

Winter Dragon leaned down and touched Warrior and Boomer, who barked and licked him in response. A chilly wind came up from behind them. "These dragons will make sure he arrives home safely. It is time you left, and if you travel at night, it will be safer for you, and you will be stronger," said Zurrum.

Winter Dragon gave a guttural goodbye and, with significant effort, flapped his wings and flew away. The two dragons followed.

"Your village is protected. We need to meet where you healed my friend." Joshua nodded.

A few of the men stayed and continued working, while the rest grabbed canoes and headed downstream. The dogs were in a canoe as soon as they touched the water. "I guess they are coming." Someone laughed.

It did not take long, with the flow of the river, to reach the spot where they had met Zurrum the previous year. Josh recognized a few of the dragons, and some of the men saw the ones they had worked with and went straight to them. Warrior ran to Ligia. They nuzzled each other, and then Zurrum spoke.

"Many things happened over the winter. Valgus, our past king, not only was he threatened by Neimacreorth but made to deliver a message to threaten me and Joshua. A message we both found unacceptable. He was told to stay in the Valley of Clouds, him and his followers. They did not. He sent many dragons to destroy these mountain people. For this, his arrogance, his evil, he must die. What do you say, Joshua?"

Josh sat, stunned at first by what Zurrum said. Someone elbowed him, and he stood up. "As you have said, Zurrum, many dragons attacked our village. If it wasn't for Winter Dragon, I am not sure we all would have survived, if any of us. We have worked on weapons over the winter. I know Neimacreorth wants to be king again, but I do have a question. You have said he can fly again."

"Yes."

"What if he can only fly short distances? What if there is another way onto that ledge? What if he doesn't come at all but just sends dragons? As you said yourself, they are safe if they stay in the Valley of Clouds, and if they aren't caught out of the valley, what can we do? This could go on for years."

Zurrum roared. Fire spit skyward, which almost killed a dragon. "What have I done?"

"There may be another way," said a soft voice. Everyone turned and looked at Ligia.

Chapter 12

They planned into the early morning. Josh could not believe it. *I'm dragon bait. Dragon bait! How did it happen? Being chief, shouldn't I get any say on this plan if Neimacreorth doesn't show up?*

"What do you think?" asked Carl.

"Your chief is a brave man. As we talked about, he is fleet of foot, and his aim with bow and arrow and spear are unequalled," said Zurrum.

"Remember, you are not alone," added Ligia.

"Thanks, all of you." *Neimacreorth, you better show up.* "We need to get back to the village." Everyone either rode on a dragon or took a canoe back.

Early the next morning, Josh woke to the village alarm. He stumbled outside and watched five dragons fly toward him and Zurrum. "Zurrum, Joshua," a dragon called out. "Neimacreorth brought in many dragons under cover of darkness and heavy clouds."

"From what I understand," said another, "they are siding with Neimacreorth because they have been wronged by men. Or have attacked man."

"This is most unfortunate," said Zurrum. "We hoped the other dragons would come and fight with us or not come at all because of the promise we made with the mountain people. Man's weapons are deadlier, but there are places we can go where man cannot. There will always be dragons, not all the types we have now, but still dragons of some kind. Let us hope the ones that survive will collaborate with man, not oppose him."

"Then we should get ready to protect your dragons and my people," said Josh as he grabbed his weapons. "Everyone, be ready for battle." He watched as the villagers moved children, animals, and food into caves and tunnels and then sprinted up to the hill.

Just as Josh reached the top of the hill, he heard a distant roaring wind. They were coming. He looked back at the village. No sign of life. Josh laid his spears down just as Warrior and Boomer arrived. "Good boys." He rubbed their necks.

The dragons were overhead. Josh held the dogs underneath the giant oak and watched the massive army. Their wings blocked the sun and whipped the grass, trees, and water, and when they roared, it vibrated like an earthquake. There were so many. It was going to be a massacre. Neimacreorth, nowhere to be seen!

He watched as the battle began. The village burned. Dragons injured or dying bellowed. Men hollered for help. The riders threw nets, arrows, and spears from off the backs of their dragons. Blood flowed everywhere. Dragons twisted around one another, spewed fire, and bit. Each tried to sink claws into vital organs.

Josh placed an arrow in his bow. He heard wings above, glanced up, and rolled out of the way just as a black dragon spit fire in his direction. He released the arrow.

No damage!

"You must be the one who fought Neimacreorth," said the black dragon as he landed across the river. "I am to send you his regards and then kill you."

"Always knew he was a coward. Forgive me if I don't give up and die. After all, I'm sure you brought help with you," said Josh

"And you brought dogs with you." A white dragon landed close by. "Don't need any more help for someone like you."

Josh placed another arrow on his bow. "You sure do talk a lot." He released it at the new dragon. Both dragons roared and flew toward Josh. "Zurrum, Ligia, help please."

Zurrum roared. "Ligia, protect Josh from Ethelinda, and I will protect him from this windbag."

Fire erupted from the four dragons. The sky exploded with a crash of thunder as Zurrum and the black dragon crashed together. Josh held a spear ready. The two beasts tangled together, necks intertwined. Each tried to break free but could not. Finally, Zurrum bit down on the black dragon's lower back and swung with his tail and knocked the dragon onto a rock. It did not seem to faze the dragon at all. It opened a small wound and a chance for Josh to throw his spear.

The thrown spear struck the beast in the right leg. Josh rolled out of the way as a tree flew in his direction. There was another crash of trees as both dragons swiped their tails at each other. "Behind you!" yelled Carl.

Josh looked back and watched two dragons, claws out, ready to breathe fire, dive toward him. "Carl, go right." Josh picked up another spear and ran toward the other dragon. "Let my aim be sure and true." The spear went deep into the dragon's throat. The dragon tried to roar but only spit up blood. Josh fired three more arrows at its heart. It fell dead at his feet.

Josh heard Carl yell. He looked up just in time to see Carl throw his axe at the dragon. The axe caught it just above the right wing. The dragon howled and landed. Carl and his wounded dragon did the same. The two proceeded to kill it. His dragon spit fire while Carl threw logs on it. Both dragons shrieked, spewed flames, while Carl yelled with each log he threw. It was horrific. The ground was blood-soaked. The acrid smell of fire was everywhere. Now the smell of burned dragons permeated the atmosphere.

"Carl, I did have some weapons left."

"We did fine. Where are Zurrum and Ligia?"

"Not sure. The dogs are gone. Hopefully, they are okay."

"Need to look after my dragon. You okay here?"

"Sure, after all, what's dragon bait for?"

Wind rustled the bushes and water, and Zurrum landed next to the mangled corpses. "You did your job well, my friend. You have been busy."

Josh looked at Zurrum's bloody body. The white stripe turned red with blood, and a deep parallel gash ran across his back. Both feet were blood-soaked. "You need help."

"The blood is not all mine. The black dragon is dead."

A screech from the village turned their attention to a small group of dragons who circled something on the ground.

"Climb on!"

Chapter 13

Without hesitation, Josh jumped on Zurrum's back. Blood soaked into his clothes from Zurrum's wounds. They sped toward the dragons.

He heard the labored breath of Carl's dragon behind them, then an earsplitting scream as they landed. Zurrum belched out fire at the closest dragon to him. Josh jumped down beside Carl.

Ligia hovered above them, holding them at bay. A net had fallen over a severely injured dragon and rider. The dragon used its wing to protect him. Warrior and Boomer were pinned under the net. They growled and snarled as they tried to chew through the rope.

"I'll get the dogs," Carl yelled.

Josh nodded and sprinted around the edge of the net. Using his sword, he sliced away the rope. Then he pulled the net over the dragon's head and body. With the wing exposed, he cut the rest of the rope away and pulled out the rider. "Couldn't leave him. Saved our lives. Take care of him."

"I will, Ashton."

A corpse shook the ground next to the dragon. They looked up to see Zurrum and Ligia being attacked by four dragons and more coming. "It's going to be a bloodbath. We have to move." Warrior had stopped growling and looked toward the mountain.

"More dragons. Looks like Guardian of the Throne," said Carl.

"You're right. Come on. Can you carry this injured man? We need to get out of here. The heat and noise are deafening. Will try and get these two injured dragons to move," yelled Josh.

The sky lit up like a firestorm. Two beasts attacked Ligia. Her albino body had splotches of red all over it. Zurrum dove up and grabbed one by the neck, then carried it straight into the firestorm and dropped it. Three Guardians attacked: one grabbed the neck, one the tail, and the third breathed fire on the exposed body. A horrific spectacle. It happened time and time again. With each explosion of thunder, pieces of dragon fell.

Dragons shook the ground like an earthquake. The stench of the dead and dying beasts penetrated the air. Wolves howled in the distance.

The fight continued in the air and on the ground.

Then silence.

Zurrum landed. "It is done."

"We will look after all the dragons we can," said Josh as he brushed away at his bloodstained clothes.

"Thank you," said Ligia. "Ethelinda went to Valley of Clouds."

Sadness fell over Zurrum. "Many dragons and people have been injured or died today. It should not have happened. We must prepare for our attack on Neimacreorth."

"It won't be easy," said Josh as he tried to take in the charred village, crushed trees, and brush. "The only tree left standing on this side of the river is the oak tree on the hill," said Josh.

"It is where we promised peace and protection between your people and mine," commented Ligia.

Troy came with potions and water. "Let me get to work."

A lone follower of Niemacreorth's slipped away.

Chapter 14

"Let's hope this works," said Josh.

"It will," Zurrum replied. "He sent the young and untrained in hopes of us being killed or injured."

Dragons snarled and growled as they feasted on dead carcasses. The noise was deafening. "Need to take dragon carcasses to the wolf packs. Don't want them in the fray," stated Josh. "Men, make sure you grab any weapons you can."

Zurrum barked out a command, and two dragons ripped off large chunks of meat to feed the wolves. The dragons were not pleased. "You will eat your fill soon enough." They went back and ate the scrapes.

Josh raised his sword where a burial site had been made. Ligia, Mystique, a Guardian, and Troy had gathered the dead warriors: both men and dragon alike. "It is time to honor the ones who died for us." The men were wrapped in blankets and placed beside a dragon. The women and children surrounded each warrior with long grass or brush. "Let us bow our heads in silence and respect for our fallen comrades," said Josh. A mournful howl from the dogs was answered by the wolves.

After a moment of silence, the grass was set on fire.

For any other scraps the dragons did not eat, the men placed in a pile, threw the broken branches, trees, wood, and anything else that would burn on it. They needed to clean up the field for the battle to come.

Later that afternoon, a signal from the mountain. "He comes, Joshua. Are you ready?" asked Zurrum.

Joshua nodded. "All right, dragon bait." Josh picked up a spear and thrust it into the ground. His wounded friends stood silent and waited.

Soon waves of thunder could be heard in the distance. Joshua watched the sky as a cloud of darkness closed in. The hurricane landed in the open field. Most flew in the air but stayed above Neimacreorth. The army was larger than the one in the morning.

"Interesting way to land," said Josh as he watched Neimacreorth descend with his bad wing extended across the back of another dragon.

"I have learned to survive. This is all that is left. You, your dogs, a worthless king, and a few wounded dragons. You are not worth my time."

"I beat you once. I will do it again."

"I am the rightful king," bellowed Neimacreorth.

Ethelinda stepped forward. "I will kill this worthless human for you." She let out an angry blast of fire.

With one fluid motion, Josh rolled to his left, pulled out the spear, and threw it at Ethelinda. The spear pierced her exposed heart. She died instantly. Neimacreoth screeched. Dead corpses came to life and took to the air with their riders.

Zurrum woke and belched out a stream of fire at Neimacreoth. A dragon landed in front of him and shielded him. It was severely wounded.

Ligia revealed herself beside Josh. "Climb on!"

"Boomer, Warrior, up." Josh jumped on Ligia and clutched the dogs and her neck as she flew back in behind the riders and across the river where the riders would come. Josh landed with her behind a pile of rocks. Troy's cloak was there. A brilliant light shone by the mountain. He had gone to help Valgus. There would be no escape to the rear.

From the front, arrows were fired; spears and nets were thrown. Guardian of the Throne were on two sides. Firestorms rippled through the sky, creating a box from which there was no escape. "It is a trap. Return to Valley," roared Neimacreoth.

Josh remembered what Zurrum had told him: Valgus light was bright like the sun. Anyone who looked at it would go blind. So, Valgus, would stay behind the army and stop Niemacreorth's dragons retreat to the valley.

He heard the dragons scream in pain as they tried to turn back. The beasts fell to the ground, hit the mountain, and were killed by weapons. Dragon riders broke off and landed safely beside Joshua. The dragons returned to the battle. While Valgus and Troy watched the rear, the frontal and side attacks began. They could only watch, and hope all went as planned.

Zurrum quickly disposed of the four dragons that had attacked him.

Neimacreorth drove forward and bellowed, "I will kill my own followers and see your worthless body dead in front of me. Then I will find and devour any humans left."

With the sound of an avalanche, the two foes crashed into each other.

The Guardians ripped apart dragons. The snarling, bone-crunching noise was deafening.

In the chaos, Josh made out the battle between the two powerful kings. Even though his wing was crippled, Neimacreorth moved easily on the ground. Both had wicked spikes on their tails that whacked the ground and swung back and forth, looking for an advantage on the blood-soaked ground. Neimacreorth crashed into Zurrum again. Zurrum slipped but regained his balance. He blasted Neimacreorth. Both roared and circled each other. Zurrum grabbed Neimacreorth's neck. In the entanglement, Zurrum was knocked off his feet. Zurrum tried to fly above Neimacreorth, but a fiery blast sent him crashing to the ground.

Neimacreorth moved forward, spikes up on his head and tail, ready to deliver the fatal blow. He lashed out at Zurrum with his tail, hitting the river instead which sent a wave of water over everyone.

Zurrum met his attack with one of his own.

Both tails swung at their opponent in hopes of doing some major injury. Zurrum caught a piece of fence and tossed it at Neimacreorth. The damage was minor but allowed Zurrum to take to the air. He attacked the injured wing. Neimacreorth shrieked.

The beast let out a steady stream of fire. Zurrum evaded it and attacked from behind, grabbed the base of the skull and tore a chunk out. Blood sprayed in the air. He stayed away from the tail and landed with his feet extended on Neimacreorth's back and ripped it open. The monster withered in pain. He twisted his neck around to grab Zurrum, but he had already flown skyward. He dove down; flames scorched the former king, then drove his clawed feet into Neimacreorth's chest. Blood gushed forth.

The ornery beast stood there defiantly, unwilling to die. It tried to make a sound, but nothing came forth. Neimacreorth died at Zurrum's feet.

Joshua and the rest of the men joined the dragons where King Zurrum stood. He held Neimacreorth's heart in his claws. "It is done."

"Like you said, it was a war that should never have happened," said Josh. The men watched as the dragons feasted on their kills. Even the dogs took part.

Most of the dragons left at Zurrum's command. Their friends took scrapes with them. Soon the only ones left were Zurrum, Ligia, Valgus, and a few Guardians.

"Thank you for your help. You are a brave chief and warrior. Without you and your men, we would not have been able to defeat Neimacreorth and his followers. I am sorry your village was destroyed. We will help you rebuild, when possible," said Zurrum.

"Thank you, my friends, for helping us get rid of someone as powerful as Neimacreorth. He killed many people. Now we are both safe. I appreciate your offer to help us rebuild our homes. It would be much appreciated." Josh took in the devastation and realized they had a lot of work to do, but if the dragons would help cut trees, it might not be such a bad job after all.

"We will leave now," Zurrum said. "My friends, we will return once we heal. Send Warrior if you need us before then." They spread their wings and disappeared into the evening sky.

A noise startled the men. They turned to see the women and children had returned from the caves. Cleanup could now begin.

CPSIA information can be obtained
at www.ICGtesting.com
Printed in the USA
BVHW070055051121
620618BV00002B/102

9 781664 110342